NOW WE ARE SIX

A. A. MILNE

Now We Are Six

WITH DECORATIONS BY

Ernest H. Shepard

A YEARLING BOOK

TO

ANNE DARLINGTON

NOW SHE IS SEVEN

AND

BECAUSE SHE IS

SO

SPESHAL

Published by
DELL PUBLISHING CO., INC.
1 Dag Hammarskjold Plaza
New York, N.Y. 10017

Reprinted by arrangement with E.P. Dutton & Co., Inc.

ISBN: 0-440-76485-8

Printed in the United States of America
Fourteenth Dell printing—November 1983

Introduction

WHEN you are reciting poetry, which is a thing we never do, you find sometimes, just as you are beginning, that Uncle John is still telling Aunt Rose that if he can't find his spectacles he won't be able to hear properly, and does she know where they are; and by the time everybody has stopped looking for them, you are at the last verse, and in another minute they will be saying, "Thank-you, thank-you," without really knowing what it was all about. So, next time, you are more careful; and, just before you begin you say, *"Er-h'r'm!"* very loudly, which means, "Now then, here we are"; and everybody stops talking and looks at you: which is what you want. So then you get in the way of saying it whenever you are asked to recite . . , and sometimes it is just as well, and sometimes it isn't. . . . And by and by you find yourself saying it without thinking. Well, this bit which I am writing now, called Introduction, is really the *er-h'r'm* of the book, and I have put it in, partly so as not to take you by surprise, and partly because I can't do without it now. There are some very clever writers who say that it is quite easy not to have an *er-h'r'm*, but I don't agree with them. I think it is much easier not to have all the rest of the book.

What I want to explain in the Introduction is this. We have been nearly three years writing this book. We began it when we were very young . . . and now we are six. So, of course, bits of it seem rather baby-ish to us, almost as if they had slipped out of some other book by mistake. On page whatever-it-is there is a thing which is simply three-ish, and when we read it to ourselves just now we said, "Well, well, well," and turned over rather quickly. So we want you to know that the name of the book doesn't mean that this is us being six all the time, but that it is about as far as we've got at present, and we half think of stopping there.

A. A. M.

P.S.—Pooh wants us to say that he thought it was a different book; and he hopes you won't mind, but he walked through it one day, looking for his friend Piglet, and sat down on some of the pages by mistake.

Contents

I have a house where I go
   When there's too many people,
I have a house where I go
   Where no one can be;
I have a house where I go,
Where nobody ever says "No";
Where no one says anything—so
   There is no one but me.

King John was not a good man—
    He had his little ways.
And sometimes no one spoke to him
    For days and days and days.
And men who came across him,
    When walking in the town,
Gave him a supercilious stare,
Or passed with noses in the air—
And bad King John stood dumbly there,
    Blushing beneath his crown.

King John was not a good man,
    And no good friends had he.
He stayed in every afternoon . . .
    But no one came to tea.
And, round about December,
    The cards upon his shelf
Which wished him lots of Christmas cheer,
And fortune in the coming year,
Were never from his near and dear,
    But only from himself.

King John was not a good man,
  Yet had his hopes and fears.
They'd given him no present now
  For years and years and years.
But every year at Christmas,
  While minstrels stood about,
Collecting tribute from the young
For all the songs they might have sung,
He stole away upstairs and hung
  A hopeful stocking out.

King John was not a good man,
  He lived his life aloof;
Alone he thought a message out
  While climbing up the roof.
He wrote it down and propped it
  Against the chimney stack:
"TO ALL AND SUNDRY—NEAR AND FAR—
F. CHRISTMAS IN PARTICULAR."
And signed it not "Johannes R."
  But very humbly, "JACK."

"I want some crackers,
    And I want some candy;
I think a box of chocolates
    Would come in handy;
I don't mind oranges,
    I do like nuts!
And I SHOULD like a pocket-knife
    That really cuts.
And, oh! Father Christmas, if you love me at all,
Bring me a big, red india-rubber ball!"

King John was not a good man—
    He wrote this message out,
And gat him to his room again,
    Descending by the spout.
And all that night he lay there,
    A prey to hopes and fears.
"I think that's him a-coming now,"
    (Anxiety bedewed his brow.)
"He'll bring one present, anyhow—
    The first I've had for years."

"Forget about the crackers,
    And forget about the candy;
I'm sure a box of chocolates
    Would never come in handy;
I don't like oranges,
    I don't want nuts,
And I HAVE got a pocket-knife
    That almost cuts.
But, oh! Father Christmas, if you love me at all,
Bring me a big, red india-rubber ball!"

King John was not a good man—
    Next morning when the sun
Rose up to tell a waiting world
    That Christmas had begun,
And people seized their stockings,
    And opened them with glee,
And crackers, toys and games appeared,
And lips with sticky sweets were smeared,
King John said grimly: "As I feared,
    Nothing again for me!"

'I did want crackers,
    And I did want candy;
I know a box of chocolates
    Would come in handy;
I do love oranges,
    I did want nuts.
I haven't got a pocket-knife—
    Not one that cuts.
And, oh! if Father Christmas had loved me at all,
He would have brought a big, red india-rubber
    ball!"

King John stood by the window,
    And frowned to see below
The happy bands of boys and girls
    All playing in the snow.
A while he stood there watching,
    And envying them all . . .
When through the window big and red
There hurtled by his royal head,
And bounced and fell upon the bed,
    An india-rubber ball!

AND, OH, FATHER CHRISTMAS,
MY BLESSINGS ON YOU FALL
    FOR BRINGING HIM
    A BIG, RED,
    INDIA-RUBBER
    BALL!

I think I am a Muffin Man. I haven't got a bell,
I haven't got the muffin things that muffin people
    sell.

Perhaps I am a Postman. No, I think I am a Tram.
I'm feeling rather funny and I don't know *what* I
    am—

          BUT
        Round about
        And *round* about
        And *round* about I go—
        All around the table,
        The table in the nursery—

Round about
And *round* about
And *round* about I go;
I think I am a Traveller escaping from a Bear;

I think I am an Elephant,
Behind another Elephant
Behind *another* Elephant who isn't really there. . . .

SO
Round about
And *round* about
And *round* about and *round* about
And *round* about
And *round* about
I go.

I think I am a Ticket Man who's selling tickets—
please,

I think I am a Doctor who is visiting a Sneeze;

Perhaps I'm just a Nanny who is walking with a
 pram
I'm feeling rather funny and I don't know *what* I
 am—

>
> **BUT**
> *Round* about
> And *round* about
> And *round* about I go—
> All around the table,
> The table in the nursery —
> *Round* about
> And *round* about
> And *round* about I go:

I think I am a Puppy, so I'm hanging out my tongue;

I think I am a Camel who
Is looking for a Camel who
Is looking for a Camel who is looking for its
    Young. . . .

             SO
         Round about
         And *round* about
         And *round* about and *round* about
         And *round* about
         And *round* about
           I go.

Christopher Robin
Had wheezles
And sneezles,
They bundled him
Into
His bed.
They gave him what goes
With a cold in the nose,
And some more for a cold
In the head.
They wondered
If wheezles
Could turn
Into measles,
If sneezles
Would turn
Into mumps;
They examined his chest
For a rash,
And the rest
Of his body for swellings and lumps.

They sent for some doctors
In sneezles
And wheezles
To tell them what ought
To be done.

All sorts and conditions
Of famous physicians
Came hurrying round
At a run.
They all made a note
Of the state of his throat,
They asked if he suffered from thirst;
They asked if the sneezles
Came *after* the wheezles,
Or if the first sneezle
Came first.
They said, "If you teazle
A sneezle
Or wheezle,
A measle
May easily grow.
But humour or pleazle
The wheezle
Or sneezle,
The measle
Will certainly go."

They expounded the reazles
For sneezles
And wheezles,
The manner of measles
When new.
They said, "If he freezles
In draughts and in breezles,
Then PHTHEEZLES
May even ensue."

Christopher Robin
Got up in the morning,
The sneezles had vanished away.
And the look in his eye
Seemed to say to the sky,
"Now, how to amuse them today?"

Binker—what I call him—is a secret of my own,
And Binker is the reason why I never feel alone.
Playing in the nursery, sitting on the stair,
Whatever I am busy at, Binker will be there.

    Oh, Daddy is clever, he's a clever sort of man,
    And Mummy is the best since the world began,
    And Nanny is Nanny, and I call her Nan—
        But they can't
        See
        Binker.

Binker's always talking, 'cos I'm teaching him to
    speak:
He sometimes likes to do it in a funny sort of
    squeak,
And he sometimes likes to do it in a hoodling sort
    of roar . . .

And I have to do it for him 'cos his throat is rather
    sore.

    Oh, Daddy is clever, he's a clever sort of man,
    And Mummy knows all that anybody can,
    And Nanny is Nanny, and I call her Nan—
        But they don't
        Know
        Binker.

Binker's brave as lions when we're running in the
    park;
Binker's brave as tigers when we're lying in the
    dark;
Binker's brave as elephants. He never, never cries
    . . .
Except (like other people) when the soap gets in his
    eyes.

Oh, Daddy is Daddy, he's a Daddy sort of man,
And Mummy is as Mummy as anybody can,
And Nanny is Nanny, and I call her Nan . . .
     But they're not
     Like
     Binker.

Binker isn't greedy, but he does like things to eat,
So I have to say to people when they're giving me
    a sweet,
"Oh, Binker wants a chocolate, so could you give
    me two?"
And then I eat it for him, 'cos his teeth are rather
    new.

Well, I'm very fond of Daddy, but he hasn't time
to play,
And I'm very fond of Mummy, but she sometimes
goes away,
And I'm often cross with Nanny when she wants to
brush my hair . . .

But Binker's always Binker, and is certain to be
there.

Tinker, Tailor,

Soldier, Sailor,

Rich Man, Poor Man,

Ploughboy,
Thief—

And what about a Cowboy,
Policeman, Jailer,
Engine-driver,
Or Pirate Chief?
What about a Postman or a Keeper at the Zoo?
What about the Circus Man who lets the people
    through?
And the man who takes the pennies for the round-
    abouts and swings,
Or the man who plays the organ, and the other
    man who sings?
What about a Conjuror with rabbits in his pockets?
What about a Rocket Man who's always making
    rockets?

Oh, there's such a lot of things to do and such a lot
    to be

That there's always lots of cherries on my little
    cherry-tree!

Of all the Knights in Appledore
    The wisest was Sir Thomas Tom.
He multiplied as far as four,
    And knew what nine was taken from
To make eleven. He could write
A letter to another Knight.

No other Knight in all the land
    Could do the things which he could do
Not only did he understand
    The way to polish swords, but knew
What remedy a Knight should seek
Whose armour had begun to squeak.

And, if he didn't fight too much,
  It wasn't that he did not care
For blips and buffetings and such,
  But felt that it was hardly fair
To risk, by frequent injuries,
A brain as delicate as his.

His castle (Castle Tom) was set
  Conveniently on a hill;
And daily, when it wasn't wet,
  He paced the battlements until
Some smaller Knight who couldn't swim
Should reach the moat and challenge him.

Or sometimes, feeling full of fight,
　　He hurried out to scour the plain;
And, seeing some approaching Knight,
　　He either hurried home again,
Or hid; and, when the foe was past,
Blew a triumphant trumpet-blast.

One day when good Sir Thomas Tom
   Was resting in a handy ditch,
The noises he was hiding from,
   Though very much the noises which
He'd always hidden from before,
Seemed somehow less. . . . Or was it more?

The trotting horse, the trumpet's blast,
   The whistling sword, the armour's squeak,
These, and especially the last,
   Had clattered by him all the week.
Was this the same, or was it not?
Something was different. But what?

Sir Thomas raised a cautious ear
   And listened as Sir Hugh went by,
And suddenly he seemed to hear
   (Or not to hear) the reason why
This stranger made a nicer sound
Than other Knights who lived around.

Sir Thomas watched the way he went—
   His rage was such he couldn't speak,
For years they'd called him down in Kent
   The Knight Whose Armour Didn't Squeak!

Yet here and now he looked upon
Another Knight whose squeak had gone.

He rushed to where his horse was tied;
  He spurred it to a rapid trot.
The only fear he felt inside
  About his enemy was not
"How sharp his sword?" "How stout his
      heart?"
  But "Has he got too long a start?"

Sir Hugh was singing, hand on hip,
  When something sudden came along,
And caught him a terrific blip
  Right in the middle of his song.
"A thunderstorm!" he thought. "Of course!"
  And toppled gently off his horse.

Then said the good Sir Thomas Tom,
　　Dismounting with a friendly air,
"Allow me to extract you from
　　The heavy armour that you wear.
At times like these the bravest Knight
May find his armour much too tight."

A hundred yards or so beyond
　　The scene of brave Sir Hugh's defeat
Sir Thomas found a useful pond,
　　And, careful not to wet his feet,
He brought the armour to the brink,
And flung it in . . . and watched it sink.

So ever after, more and more,
    The men of Kent would proudly speak
Of Thomas Tom of Appledore,
    "The Knight Whose Armour Didn't Squeak'
Whilst Hugh, the Knight who gave him best,
Squeaks just as badly as the rest.

Where is Anne?
   Head above the buttercups,
Walking by the stream,
   Down among the buttercups.
Where is Anne?
Walking with her man,
Lost in a dream,
   Lost among the buttercups.

What has she got in that little brown head?
Wonderful thoughts which can never be said.
What has she got in that firm little fist of hers?
Somebody's thumb, and it feels like Christopher's.

   Where is Anne?
   Close to her man.
   Brown head, gold head,
     In and out the buttercups.

The charcoal-burner has tales to tell.
He lives in the Forest,
Alone in the Forest;
He sits in the Forest,
Alone in the Forest.
And the sun comes slanting between the trees,
And rabbits come up, and they give him good-
     morning,
And rabbits come up and say, "Beautiful morn-
     ing" . . .
And the moon swings clear of the tall black trees,
And owls fly over and wish him good-night,
Quietly over to wish him good-night . . .

And he sits and thinks of the things they know,
He and the Forest, alone together—
The springs that come and the summers that go,
Autumn dew on bracken and heather,
The drip of the Forest beneath the snow . . .

All the things they have seen,
All the things they have heard:
An April sky swept clean and the song of a bird . .

Oh, the charcoal-burner has tales to tell!
And he lives in the Forest and knows us well.

Wherever I am, there's always Pooh,
There's always Pooh and Me.
Whatever I do, he wants to do,
"Where are you going today?" says Pooh:
"Well, that's very odd 'cos I was too.
Let's go together," says Pooh, says he.
"Let's go together," says Pooh.

"What's twice eleven?" I said to Pooh.
("Twice what?" said Pooh to Me.)
"I *think* it ought to be twenty-two."
"Just what I think myself," said Pooh.
"It wasn't an easy sum to do,
But that's what it is," said Pooh, said he.
"That's what it is," said Pooh.

"Let's look for dragons," I said to Pooh.
"Yes, let's," said Pooh to Me.
  We crossed the river and found a few—
"Yes, those are dragons all right," said Pooh.
"As soon as I saw their beaks I knew.
  That's what they are," said Pooh, said he.
"That's what they are," said Pooh.

"Let's frighten the dragons,"I said to Pooh.
"That's right," said Pooh to Me.
"*I'm* not afraid," I said to Pooh,
  And I held his paw and I shouted "Shoo!
  Silly old dragons!"—and off they flew.
"I wasn't afraid," said Pooh, said he,
"I'm *never* afraid with you."

So wherever I am, there's always Pooh,
    There's always Pooh and Me.
"What would I do?" I said to Pooh,
"If it wasn't for you," and Pooh said: "True,
    It isn't much fun for One, but Two
    Can stick together," says Pooh, says he.
"That's how it is," says Pooh.

There was once an old sailor my grandfather knew
Who had so many things which he wanted to do
That, whenever he thought it was time to begin,
He couldn't because of the state he was in.

He was shipwrecked, and lived on an island for
weeks,

And he wanted a hat,

and he wanted some breeks;

And he wanted some nets, or a line and some hooks
For the turtles and things which you read of in
    books.

And, thinking of this, he remembered a thing
Which he wanted (for water) and that was a spring;
And he thought that to talk to he'd look for, and
    keep
(If he found it) a goat, or some chickens and sheep.

Then, because of the weather, he wanted a hut
With a door (to come in by) which opened and shut
(With a jerk, which was useful if snakes were about),
And a very strong lock to keep savages out.

He began on the fish-hooks, and when he'd begun
He decided he couldn't because of the sun.

So he knew what he ought to begin with, and that
Was to find, or to make, a large sun-stopping hat.

He was making the hat with some leaves from a
    tree,
When he thought, "I'm as hot as a body can be,
And I've nothing to take for my terrible thirst;
So I'll look for a spring, and I'll look for it *first*."

Then he thought as he started, "Oh, dear and oh,
    dear!
I'll be lonely tomorrow with nobody here!"
So he made in his note-book a couple of notes:
"I must first find some chickens"

and *"No, I mean goats."*

He had just seen a goat (which he knew by the
    shape)
When he thought, "But I must have a boat for
    escape.

But a boat means a sail, which means needles and
    thread;
So I'd better sit down and make needles instead."

He began on a needle, but thought as he worked,
That, if this was an island where savages lurked,
Sitting safe in his hut he'd have nothing to fear,
Whereas now they might suddenly breathe in his
ear!

So he thought of his hut . . . and he thought of
his boat,
And his hat and his breeks, and his chickens and
goat,
And the hooks (for his food) and the spring (for his
thirst) . . .
But he *never* could think which he ought to do first.

And so in the end he did nothing at all,
But basked on the shingle wrapped up in a shawl.
And I think it was dreadful the way he behaved—
He did nothing but basking until he was saved!

Let it rain!
Who cares?
I've a train
Upstairs,
With a brake
Which I make
From a string
Sort of thing,
Which works
In jerks,
'Cos it drops
In the spring,
Which stops
With the string,

And the wheels
All stick
So quick
That it feels
Like a thing
That you make
With a brake,
Not string. . . .

So that's what I make,
When the day's all wet.
It's a good sort of brake
But it hasn't worked yet.

Christopher, Christopher, where are you going,
                              Christopher Robin?
    "Just up to the top of the hill,
    Upping and upping until
    I am right on the top of the hill,"
                    Said Christopher Robin.

Christopher, Christopher, why are you going,
            Christopher Robin?
There's nothing to see, so when
You've got to the top, what then?
"Just down to the bottom again,"
            Said Christopher Robin.

If I were a bear,
  And a big bear too,
I shouldn't much care
  If it froze or snew;
I shouldn't much mind
  If it snowed or friz—
I'd be all fur-lined
  With a coat like his!

For I'd have fur boots and a brown fur wrap,
And brown fur knickers and a big fur cap.
I'd have a fur muffle-ruff to cover my jaws,
And brown fur mittens on my big brown paws.
With a big brown furry-down up to my head,
I'd sleep all the winter in a big fur bed.

I found a little beetle, so that Beetle was his name,
And I called him Alexander and he answered just
    the same.
I put him in a match-box, and I kept him all the
    day . . .
And Nanny let my beetle out—

Yes, Nanny let my beetle out—

She went and let my beetle out—

And Beetle ran away.

She said she didn't mean it,
    and I never said she did,
She said she wanted matches
    and she just took off
    the lid,

She said that she was sorry, but it's difficult to catch
An excited sort of beetle you've mistaken for a
    match.

She said that she was sorry, and I really mustn't
    mind,
As there's lots and lots of beetles which she's cer-
    tain we could find,
If we looked about the garden for the holes where
    beetles hid—
And we'd get another match-box and write
    BEETLE on the lid.

We went to all the places which a beetle might be
    near,
And we made the sort of noises which a beetle
    likes to hear,
And I saw a kind of something, and I gave a sort
    of shout:
"A beetle-house and Alexander Beetle coming out!"

It was Alexander Beetle I'm as certain as can be
And he had a sort of look as if he thought it must
be ME,

And he had a sort of look as if he thought he ought
to say:
"I'm very, very sorry that I tried to run away."

And Nanny's very sorry too for you-know-what-she-
did,
And she's writing ALEXANDER very blackly on
the lid.
So Nan and Me are friends, because it's difficult to
catch
An excited Alexander you've mistaken for a match.

The King of **Peru**
(Who was Emperor too)
    Had a sort of a rhyme
        Which was useful to know,
If he felt very shy
When a stranger came by,
    Or they asked him the time
        When his watch didn't go:
Or supposing he fell
(By mistake) down a well,
    Or he tumbled when skating
    And sat on his hat,
Or perhaps wasn't told,
Till his porridge was cold,
    That his breakfast was waiting—
        Or something like that;

Oh, whenever the Emperor
Got into a temper, or
   Felt himself sulky or sad,
He would murmur and murmur,
Until he felt firmer,
   This curious rhyme which he had:

Eight eights are sixty-four;
   Multiply by seven.
When it's done,
Carry one,
   And take away eleven.
Nine nines are eighty-one;
   Multiply by three.
If it's more,
Carry four,
   And then it's time for tea.

So whenever the Queen
Took his armour to clean,
    And she didn't remember
      To use any starch;
Or his birthday (in May)
Was a horrible day,
    Being wet as November
      And windy as March;
Or, if sitting in state
With the Wise and the Great,
    He just happened to hiccup
      While signing his name,
Or the Queen gave a cough,
When his crown tumbled off
    As he bent down to pick up
      A pen for the same;

Oh, whenever the Emperor
Got into a temper, or
    Felt himself awkward and shy,

He would whisper and whisper,
Until he felt crisper,
  This odd little rhyme to the sky:

Eight eights are eighty-one;
  Multiply by seven.
If it's more,
Carry four,
  And take away eleven.
Nine nines are sixty-four;
  Multiply by three.
When it's done,
Carry one,
  And then it's time for tea.

Whenever I'm a shining Knight,
I buckle on my armour tight;
And then I look about for things,
Like Rushings-Out, and Rescuings,
And Savings from the Dragon's Lair,
And fighting all the Dragons there.
And sometimes when our fights begin,
I think I'll let the Dragons win . . .
And then I think perhaps I won't,
Because they're Dragons, and I don't.

There's sun on the river and sun on the hill . . .
You can hear the sea if you stand quite still!
There's eight new puppies at Roundabout Farm—
And I saw an old sailor with only one arm!

But every one says, "Run along!"
(Run along, run along!)
All of them say, "Run along! I'm busy as can be."
Every one says, "Run along,
There's a little darling!"
If I'm a little darling, why don't they run with me?

There's wind on the river and wind on the hill . . .
There's a dark dead water-wheel under the mill!
I saw a fly which had just been drowned—
And I know where a rabbit goes into the ground!

But every one says, "Run along!"
(Run along, run along!)
All of them say, "Yes, dear," and never notice me.
Every one says, "Run along,
There's a little darling!"
If I'm a little darling, why won't they come and see?

I'm fishing.
Don't talk, anybody, don't come near!
Can't you see that the fish might hear?
He thinks I'm playing with a piece of string;
He thinks I'm another sort of funny sort of thing,
    But he doesn't know I'm fishing—
    He doesn't know I'm fishing.
        That's what I'm doing—
            Fishing.

No, I'm not, I'm newting.
Don't cough, anybody, don't come by!
Any small noise makes a newt feel shy.
He thinks I'm a bush, or a new sort of tree;
He thinks it's somebody, but doesn't think it's Me,
    And he doesn't know I'm newting—
    No, he doesn't know I'm newting.
        That's what I'm doing—
            Newting.

Berryman and Baxter,
    Prettiboy and Penn
And old Farmer Middleton
    Are five big men . . .
And all of them were after
    The Little Black Hen.

She ran quickly,
    They ran fast;
Baxter was first, and
    Berryman was last.
I sat and watched
    By the old plum-tree . . .
She squawked through the hedge
    And she came to me.

The Little Black Hen
  Said "Oh, it's you!"
I said "Thank you,
  How do you do?
And please will you tell me,
  Little Black Hen,
What did they want,
  Those five big men?"

The Little Black Hen
  She said to me:
"They want me to lay them
  An egg for tea.
If they were Emperors,
  If they were Kings.
I'm much too busy
  To lay them things."

"I'm not a King
    And I haven't a crown;
I climb up trees,
    And I tumble down.
I can shut one eye,
    I can count to ten,
So lay me an egg, please,
    Little Black Hen."

The Little Black Hen said,
    "What will you pay,
If I lay you an egg
    For Easter Day?"

"I'll give you a Please
    And a How-do-you-do,
I'll show you the Bear
    Who lives in the Zoo,
I'll show you the nettle-place
    On my leg,
If you'll lay me a great big
    Eastery egg."

The Little Black Hen
  Said "I don't care
For a How-do-you-do
  Or a Big-brown-bear,
But I'll lay you a beautiful
  Eastery egg,
If you'll show me the nettle-place
  On your leg."

I showed her the place
  Where I had my sting.
She touched it gently
  With one black wing.
"Nettles don't hurt
  If you count to ten.
And now for the egg,"
  Said the Little Black Hen.

When I wake up
   On Easter Day,
I shall see my egg
   She's promised to lay.
If I were Emperors,
   If I were Kings,
It couldn't be fuller
   Of wonderful things.

Berryman and Baxter,
   Prettiboy and Penn,
And Old Farmer Middleton
   Are five big men.
All of them are wanting
   An egg for their tea,
But the Little Black Hen is much too busy,
The Little Black Hen is *much* too busy,
The Little Black Hen is MUCH too busy . .
   She's laying my egg for me!

There are lots and lots of people who are always
    asking things,
Like Dates and Pounds-and-ounces and the names
    of funny Kings,
And the answer's either Sixpence or A Hundred
    Inches Long,
And I know they'll think me silly if I get the an-
    swer wrong.

So Pooh and I go whispering, and Pooh looks very
    bright,
And says, "Well, *I* say sixpence, but I don't suppose
    I'm right."
And then it doesn't matter what the answer ought
    to be,
'Cos if he's right, I'm Right, and if he's wrong, it
    isn't Me.

It's funny how often they say to me, "Jane?
  "Have you been a *good* girl?"
  "Have you been a *good* girl?"
And when they have said it, they say it again,
  "Have you been a *good* girl?"
  "Have you been a *good* girl?"

I go to a party, I go out to tea,
I go to an aunt for a week at the sea,
I come back from school or from playing a game;
Wherever I come from, it's always the same:
  "Well?
  Have you been a *good* girl, Jane?"

It's always the end of the loveliest day:
  "Have you been a *good* girl?"
  "Have you been a *good* girl?"
I went to the Zoo, and they waited to say:
  "Have you been a *good* girl?"
  "Have you been a *good* girl?"

Well, what did they think that I went there to do?
And why should I want to be bad at the Zoo?
And should I be likely to say if I had?
So that's why it's funny of Mummy and Dad,
This asking and asking, in case I was bad,
  "Well?
    Have you been a *good* girl, Jane?"

If I were John and John were Me,
Then he'd be six and I'd be three.
If John were Me and I were John,
I shouldn't have these trousers on.

Of Hilary the Great and Good
>   *They tell a tale at Christmas time*
I've often thought the story would
Be prettier but just as good
If almost anybody should
>   *Translate it into rime.*
So I have done the best I can
For lack of some more learned man.

   Good King Hilary
   Said to his Chancellor
   (Proud Lord Willoughby,
   Lord High Chancellor):
"Run to the wicket-gate
   Quickly, quickly,
   Run to the wicket-gate
      And see who is knocking.
   It may be a rich man,
   Sea-borne from Araby,
   Bringing me peacocks,
   Emeralds and ivory;
   It may be a poor man,
   Travel-worn and weary,
   Bringing me oranges
      To put in my stocking."

Proud Lord Willoughby,
Lord High Chancellor,
  Laughed both loud and free:*
"I've served Your Majesty, man to man,
Since first Your Majesty's reign began,
And I've often walked, but I never, never ran,
  Never, never, never," quoth he.

Good King Hilary
Said to his Chancellor
(Proud Lord Willoughby,
Lord High Chancellor):
"Walk to the wicket-gate
Quickly, quickly,
Walk to the wicket-gate
  And see who is knocking.

  * Haw! Haw! Haw!

It may be a captain,
Hawk-nosed, bearded,
Bringing me gold-dust,
Spices, and sandalwood:

It may be a scullion,
Care-free, whistling,
Bringing me sugar-plums
    To put in my stocking."

Proud Lord Willoughby,
Lord High Chancellor,
    Laughed both loud and free:
"I've served in the Palace since I was four,
And I'll serve in the Palace a-many years more,
And I've opened a window, but never a door,
    Never, never, never," quoth he.

Good King Hilary
Said to his Chancellor
(Proud Lord Willoughby,
Lord High Chancellor):
"Open the window
Quickly, quickly,
Open the window
      And see who is knocking.

It may be a waiting-maid,
Apple-cheeked, dimpled,
Sent by her mistress
To bring me greeting;
It may be children,
Anxious, whispering,
Bringing me cobnuts,
      To put in my stocking."

Proud Lord Willoughby,
Lord High Chancellor,
     Laughed both loud and free;
'I'll serve Your Majesty till I die—
As Lord Chancellor, not as spy
To peep from lattices; no, not I,
     Never, never, never," quoth he.

Good King Hilary
Looked at his Chancellor
(Proud Lord Willoughby,
Lord High Chancellor):
He said no word
To his stiff-set Chancellor,
But ran to the wicket-gate
     To see who was knocking.
He found no rich man
Trading from Araby;
He found no captain,
Blue-eyed, weather-tanned;
He found no waiting-maid
Sent by her mistress;
But only a beggarman
     With one red stocking.

Good King Hilary
Looked at the beggarman,
     And laughed him three times three;

And he turned that beggarman round about:
"Your thews are strong, and your arm is stout;
Come, throw me a Lord High Chancellor
    out,
        And take his place," quoth he.

Of Hilary the Good and Great
Old wives at Christmas time relate
This tale, which points, at any rate,
        Two morals on the way.
The first: *"Whatever Fortune brings,
Don't be afraid of doing things."*
(Especially, of course, for Kings.)
        It also seems to say
(But not so wisely): *"He who begs
With one red stocking on his legs
Will be, as sure as eggs are eggs,
        A Chancellor some day."*

Here I go up in my swing
   Ever so high.
I am the King of the fields, and the King
   Of the town.
I am the King of the earth, and the King
   Of the sky.
Here I go up in my swing . . .
   Now I go down.

Elizabeth Ann
Said to her Nan:
"Please will you tell me how God began?
Somebody must have made Him. So
Who could it be, 'cos I want to know?"
And Nurse said, "*Well!*"
And Ann said, "Well?
I know you know, and I wish you'd tell."
And Nurse took pins from her mouth, and said,
"Now then, darling, it's time for bed."

Elizabeth Ann
Had a wonderful plan:
She would run round the world till she found a
      man
Who knew *exactly* how God began.

She got up early, she dressed, and ran
Trying to find an Important Man.
She ran to London and knocked at the door
Of the Lord High Doodelum's coach-and-four.
"Please, sir (if there's anyone in),
However-and-ever did God begin?"

The Lord High Doodelum lay in bed,

But out of the window, large and red,
Came the Lord High Coachman's face instead.
And the Lord High Coachman laughed and
    said:
"Well, what put *that* in your quaint little
    head?"

Elizabeth Ann went home again
And took from the ottoman Jennifer Jane.
"Jenniferjane," said Elizabeth Ann,
"Tell me *at once* how God began."
And Jane, who didn't much care for speaking,
Replied in her usual way by squeaking.

What did it mean? Well, to be quite candid,
I don't know, but Elizabeth Ann did.
Elizabeth Ann said softly, "Oh!
Thank you, Jennifer. Now I know."

There were Two little Bears who lived in a Wood,
And one of them was Bad and the other was Good.
Good Bear learnt his Twice Times One—
But Bad Bear left all his buttons undone.

They lived in a Tree when the weather was hot,
And one of them was Good, and the other was Not.
Good Bear learnt his Twice Times Two—
But Bad Bear's thingummies were worn right
    through.

They lived in a Cave when the weather was cold,
And they Did, and they Didn't Do, what they were
    told.
Good Bear learnt his Twice Times Three—
But Bad Bear *never* had his hand-ker-chee.

They lived in the Wood with a Kind Old Aunt,
And one said "Yes'm," and the other said "Shan't!"
Good Bear learnt his Twice Times Four—
But Bad Bear's knicketies were terrible tore.

And then quite suddenly (just like Us)
One got Better and the other got Wuss.
Good Bear muddled his Twice Times Three—
But Bad Bear coughed *in his hand-ker-chee!*

Good Bear muddled his Twice Times Two—
But Bad Bear's thingummies looked like new.
Good Bear muddled his Twice Times One—
But Bad Bear *never* left his buttons undone.

There may be a Moral, though some say not;
I think there's a moral, though I don't know what.
But if one gets better, as the other gets wuss,
These Two Little Bears are just like Us.
For Christopher remembers up to Twice Times
    Ten . . .
But I keep forgetting where I've put my pen.*

* *So I have had to write this one in pencil.*

When Anne and I go out a walk,
We hold each other's hand and talk
Of all the things we mean to do
When Anne and I are forty-two.

And when we've thought about a thing,
Like bowling hoops or bicycling,
Or falling down on Anne's balloon,
We do it in the afternoon.

O Timothy Tim
   Has ten pink toes,
   And ten pink toes
Has Timothy Tim.
They go with him
   Wherever he goes,
   And wherever he goes
They go with him.

O Timothy Tim
   Has two blue eyes,
   And two blue eyes
Has Timothy Tim.
They cry with him
   Whenever he cries,
   And whenever he cries,
They cry with him.

O Timothy Tim
   Has one red head,
   And one red head.
Has Timothy Tim.
It sleeps with him
   In Timothy's bed.
   Sleep well, red head
Of Timothy Tim.

These are my two drops of rain
Waiting on the window-pane.

I am waiting here to see
Which the winning one will be.

Both of them have different names.
One is John and one is James.

All the best and all the worst
Comes from which of them is first.

James has just begun to ooze.
He's the one I want to lose.

John is waiting to begin.
He's the one I want to win.

James is going slowly on.
Something sort of sticks to John.

John is moving off at last.
James is going pretty fast.

John is rushing down the pane.
James is going slow again.

James has met a sort of smear.
John is getting very near.

Is he going fast enough?
(James has found a piece of fluff.)

John has hurried quickly by.
(James was talking to a fly.)

John is there, and John has won!
Look! I told you! Here's the sun!

Tattoo was the mother of Pinkle Purr,
A little black nothing of feet and fur;
And by-and-by, when his eyes came through,
He saw his mother, the big Tattoo.
And all that he learned he learned from her.
"I'll ask my mother," says Pinkle Purr.

Tattoo was the mother of Pinkle Purr,
A ridiculous kitten with silky fur.
And little black Pinkle grew and grew
Till he got as big as the big Tattoo.
And all that he did he did with her.
"Two friends together," says Pinkle Purr.

Tattoo was the mother of Pinkle Purr,
An adventurous cat in a coat of fur.
And whenever he thought of a thing to do,
He didn't much bother about Tattoo,
For he knows it's nothing to do with her,
So "See you later," says Pinkle Purr.

Tattoo is the mother of Pinkle Purr,
An enormous leopard with coal-black fur.
A little brown kitten that's nearly new
Is now playing games with its big Tattoo . . .
And Pink looks lazily down at her:
"Dear little Tat," says Pinkle Purr.

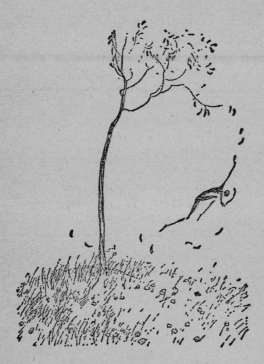

No one can tell me,
    Nobody knows,
Where the wind comes from,
    Where the wind goes.

It's flying from somewhere
  As fast as it can,
I couldn't keep up with it,
  Not if I ran.

But if I stopped holding
  The string of my kite,
It would blow with the wind
  For a day and a night.

And then when I found it,
  Wherever it blew,
I should know that the wind
  Had been going there too.

So then I could tell them
  Where the wind goes . . .
But where the wind comes from
  Nobody knows.

Lords of the Nursery
  Wait in a row,
Five on the high wall,
  And four on the low;
Big Kings and Little Kings,
  Brown Bears and Black,
All of them waiting
  Till John comes back.

Some think that John boy
  Is lost in the wood,
Some say he couldn't be,
  Some say he could.
Some think that John boy
  Hides on the hill;
Some say he won't come back,
  Some say he will.

High was the sun, when
   John went away . . .
Here they've been waiting
   All through the day;
Big Bears and Little Bears,
   White Kings and Black,
All of them waiting
   Till John comes back.

Lords of the Nursery
   Looked down the hill,
Some saw the sheep-fold,
   Some saw the mill;
Some saw the roofs
   Of the little grey town . . .
And their shadows grew long
   As the sun slipt down.

Gold between the poplars
  An old moon shows;
Silver up the star-way
  The full moon rose;
Silver down the star-way
  The old moon crept . . .
And, one by another,
  The grey fields slept.

Lords of the Nursery
  Their still watch keep . . .
They hear from the sheep-fold
  The rustle of sheep.
A young bird twitters
  And hides its head;
A little wind suddenly
  Breathes, and is dead.

Slowly and slowly
  Dawns the new day . . .
What's become of John boy?.

No one can say.
Some think that John boy
  Is lost on the hill;
Some say he won't come back,
  Some say he will.

What's become of John boy?
  Nothing at all,
He played with his skipping rope,
  He played with his ball.
He ran after butterflies,
  Blue ones and red;
He did a hundred happy things—
  And then went to bed.

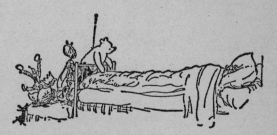

I've had my supper,
  And *had* my supper,
    And *HAD* my supper and all;
I've heard the story
  Of Cinderella,
    And how she went to the ball;
I've cleaned my teeth,
  And I've said my prayers,
    And I've cleaned and said them right;
And they've all of them been
  And kissed me lots,
    They've all of them said "Good-night."

So—here I am in the dark alone,
  There's nobody here to see;

I think to myself,
I play to myself,
And nobody knows what I say to myself;
Here I am in the dark alone,
What is it going to be?
I can think whatever I like to think,
I can play whatever I like to play,
I can laugh whatever I like to laugh,
There's nobody here but me.

I'm talking to a rabbit . . .
I'm talking to the sun . . .

I think I am a hundred—
    I'm one.
I'm lying in a forest . . .
    I'm lying in a cave . . .
I'm talking to a Dragon . . .
    I'm BRAVE.
I'm lying on my left side . . .
    I'm lying on my right . . .
I'll play a lot tomorrow . . .
    · · · · · · ·

I'll think a lot tomorrow . . .
    · · · · · · ·

I'll laugh . . .

            a lot . . .
              tomorrow . . .
            (Heigh-ho!)
                Good-night.

When I was One,
I had just begun.

When I was Two,
I was nearly new.

When I was Three,
I was hardly Me.

When I was Four,
I was not much more.

When I was Five,
I was just alive.

But now I am Six, I'm as clever as clever.
So I think I'll be six now for ever and ever.